Also by Rachael Reed

Sis
Sis 2 Blood on the Streets

Standalone
Codefendant
Codefendant
Once a Cheater
Once a Cheater
Passport Bro
What Happens in Prison
Preference
Sprinkle Sprinkle
Championship Bad
Street Exodus
Street Exodus
Street Royalty
Pawns of Power
SIS
Cartel Bloodline
Get Money Girls
Skip the Games
Til Death Do Us Part

Backpage Hustle
Link in Bio
The Virgin and The Kingpin
A Gangsta's Heart
Boosters
Can't Turn a Hoe Into a Housewife
Better you Than Me
Wig Dealer: How to Start Your wig Business
Trail Ride Blues
Demure Diva
Queen of the Carnival
Caribbean Carnival Hoe
How to Glow Up! Make 2025 Your Best Year
How to Lose 10 Pounds in a Month
What is Project 2025? The Easy to Understand Guide
What Is A Tariff
Natural Hair Growth Oil with 50 Recipes
Regrow Hair Naturally in 3 Weeks
Hustlin Through the Holidays

Hustlin' Through the Holidays

Rachael Reed
© 2024

Hustlin Through The Holidays

By TBDB PUBLISHING

Copyright © 2024 by Rachael Reed

Chapter 1: Notice on the Door

Jasmine was starting her day, the thin blanket barely covering her body as the icy draft from the busted window crept in. The kids were still asleep, their tiny bodies bundled together on the pullout couch. Her mattress on the floor wasn't much better, springs poking through, but it was the least of her problems. She rubbed her eyes and dragged herself to her feet, the weight of exhaustion pulling at her limbs. Two jobs, double shifts, and it still felt like she was running in quicksand.

Her slippers scuffed across the cold floor as she shuffled to the door. A loud knock had startled her awake earlier, but she'd ignored it, too tired to care. Now, curiosity tugged at her. She pulled open the door and froze. A bright red eviction notice flapped against the chipped wood.

"Shit," she muttered, snatching it off. Her heart pounded as she read the bold letters: **FINAL NOTICE.** Rent due in full by the 20th or she and her kids would be out on the streets.

Tears stung her eyes, but she blinked them away. Cryin' ain't gon' fix shit, she thought, slamming the door shut. The kids starting to stretch and wake up on the couch, she forced herself to push the panic down, bury it deep like she always did.

"Momma, we got cereal?" her youngest, Nia, asked, rubbing her sleepy eyes.

Jasmine plastered on a smile. "Yeah, baby, go sit at the table. I'ma fix y'all somethin.'"

The truth? There wasn't enough milk to cover the bottom of the bowl. She poured the last bit over some stale cornflakes and slid it across the table. Her oldest, Dre, frowned but didn't say nothin'. He was only ten but had already seen enough to know better than to complain.

Jasmine's stomach growled, but she ignored it. She hadn't eaten since her shift at the club last night. Instead, she busied herself, straightening the tiny apartment. The lights flickered again, a reminder that the power bill was overdue. Another shut-off notice was sitting on the counter, daring her to open it.

Her phone buzzed, and she snatched it up, hoping for some good news. Instead, it was a text from her landlord, Mr. Collins, asking when she'd have the rent. He was a sleazy bastard, always leering at her when she walked by. He'd already hinted more than once that he'd "work somethin' out" if she spent some time alone with him.

"Never that," she muttered, tossing the phone aside.

She got the kids ready and sent off to school and they started the day as usual. The neighborhood was buzzing as she walked to her first job. The old heads sat on their stoops, chain-smoking and talking shit, while the young girls with tight leggings and cheap wigs strutted past, pretending not to hear the catcalls. Jasmine kept her head down, moving fast.

She caught snatches of gossip as she passed:

"Girl, you hear Jasmine strugglin' again?"

"She always strugglin'. Them jobs ain't enough for them kids."

"At least she workin'. Half y'all baby daddies don't even"

Jasmine turned the corner, drowning out the noise. She'd heard it all before: the pity, the judgment, the sideways glances. She didn't have time to care.

The office building where she cleaned was eerily quiet in the early morning. Jasmine tied a bandana over her hair and got to work, scrubbing floors and emptying trash cans. The bleach burned her nostrils, but at least the motion gave her time to think.

How was she gonna come up with the rent in two weeks? Her tips at the club were barely enough to cover food. She'd already pawned the TV, her grandmother's bracelet, and anything else worth money.

The answer came later that night, though Jasmine didn't know it yet.

Her second job at the club was always a shitshow. The men were either broke, drunk, or both. She carried trays of watered-down drinks, dodging hands and fake smiles. Her boss, Rico, leaned against the bar, his eyes tracking her every move.

"You movin' slow tonight, Jas. You good?" he asked.

"I'm fine," she lied, slamming a tray of empties onto the bar.

After her shift, she was too tired to take the bus, so she walked home through the strip mall to save the fare. That's when she saw them two girls, barely older than her, sitting in the food court. One was flipping through a wad of cash so thick it made Jasmine's mouth dry.

"I'm tellin' you, them LV bags was a score," the girl with the bright red wig said.

"Shit, I told you. Them rich folks don't even notice half the time," her friend replied, popping gum. "You just gotta move quick, be slick with it."

Jasmine paused, pretending to adjust her shoe, but her ears were locked in.

"They got cameras everywhere, though," Red Wig said.

"Yeah, but who lookin'? Half them guards don't even care."

The girls laughed, loud and carefree, as they counted their money.

Jasmine's mind raced as she walked home. Shoplifting? She'd never even considered it. She was barely comfortable sneaking extra ketchup packets from McDonald's. But the way they talked, it sounded... easy.

By the time she got home, the idea had burrowed deep. She got the kids ready for bed tucked them in, kissed their foreheads, and sat in the dark, staring at the eviction notice.

Maybe, just maybe, she could pull it off. One hit. Enough to get Mr. Collins off her back and keep her kids warm through Christmas.

Her heart pounded as she imagined it. The thrill, the risk. She didn't want to be that girl, the one running schemes to survive. But what choice did she have?

"God, forgive me," she whispered.

The streets outside her window were alive with the usual chaos sirens wailing, dogs barking, someone arguing loudly in the distance. Jasmine leaned back against the wall, gripping the eviction notice in one hand and her phone in the other.

Tomorrow, she'd go back to that strip mall. Not to clean, but to learn.

Jasmine sat on the edge of her beat-up couch, bouncing her knee nervously. The kids were asleep, the apartment dim except for the flickering light of the cracked TV. She stared at the eviction notice on the coffee table, the bold red letters screaming at her. Her stomach churned.

"Shit, Jas, what the hell you doin'?" she muttered to herself, gripping her head.

Her plan felt shaky, risky, but the sound of her kids breathing in the next room reminded her why she had to try. No landlord was gonna put her babies on the street. She grabbed her hoodie and tucked her wild curls into a messy bun. She wasn't gonna be that chick caught slippin'.

The strip mall gleamed under harsh fluorescent lights, Christmas decorations and sparkling displays. Jasmine swallowed hard as she walked, her heart racing like she'd already been caught. She felt like everyone could see her like a big, red target was on her back.

"Act normal, girl. Ain't nobody lookin' at you," she whispered to herself, adjusting her hoodie.

She headed toward the high-end section of the mall, where the expensive stores lined up like promises she couldn't afford. Louis Vuitton, Gucci, Prada all taunting her with displays of wealth she'd never touch legit. Her fingers brushed against the strap of her fake designer purse, the knockoff stitching a glaring reminder of the life she lived.

Jasmine scoped the store like she belonged there, even though she didn't. The saleslady was busy with a bougie couple, some old white dude and his much younger girl, their loud laughs filling the space. Perfect distraction.

She moved toward the shelves, her eyes locking onto a black-and-gold bag that screamed money. The price tag dangling off it read $2,800. Her chest tightened.

"All right, Jas. You got this. In and out, nobody gon' notice," she whispered under her breath.

She grabbed the bag with shaking hands, trying to make it look casual, like she was just browsing. Her palms were sweaty as she slipped the strap over her shoulder and moved toward the exit.

The alarms didn't go off.

Jasmine couldn't believe it. She was outside, her heart hammering so loud it drowned out everything else. She gripped the bag tight, her breathing shallow. She forced herself to walk casually, even though her legs felt like jelly.

Once she hit the parking lot, she ducked into an alley and leaned against the wall, the cold bricks pressing into her back. She clutched the bag to her chest, a rush of adrenaline surging through her.

"I did it," she muttered, her voice shaking. "I really did that shit."

But the high didn't last long. Paranoia set in fast. She scanned the street for cops, security, anyone who might've seen her. The world felt too loud, too big, and she was just waiting for the other shoe to drop.

Jasmine knew who to call. Marcus, a hustler who'd been in the game for years, had a reputation for moving stolen goods quick. His name came up whenever people talked about makin' fast cash. She dialed his number, her fingers trembling as she typed.

"Yo, who dis?" his deep voice answered after a few rings.

"It's Jasmine. Tameka's girl. I need you to help me move somethin.'"

"Aight, Jas. Whatchu got?"

"A bag. Louis Vuitton. Brand new."

Marcus paused, then chuckled. "You boostin' now, huh? Didn't think you had it in you."

"Just tryna keep my lights on," she snapped, her tone sharper than she intended.

"Chill, ma. Bring it by my spot. I'll take a look."

Marcus's place was tucked behind a convenience store, his apartment a maze of mismatched furniture and stacks of stolen goods. He greeted her with a sly grin, his gold tooth glinting in the dim light.

"Lemme see," he said, holding out his hand.

Jasmine pulled the bag from under her hoodie and placed it on the table. Marcus whistled low, turning it over in his hands like he was inspecting a diamond.

"This nice. Real nice. I can give you five for it."

"Five hundred?" she asked, her voice barely above a whisper.

"Yeah. Cash. You want more, you gon' have to start buildin' a stash. Bigger loads, bigger payouts."

Jasmine nodded, her mouth dry. Five hundred was more than she'd seen in weeks.

"Deal," she said, her voice steady.

Marcus handed her a stack of crumpled bills, and she tucked it into her pocket like it was life itself.

"You seem good at this," he said, smirking. "If you ever wanna step it up, hit me up. Streets always need a good plug."

Jasmine didn't respond. She wasn't about to make this her life. This was a one-time thing.

The walk home felt lighter, but the weight of what she'd done still pressed on her chest. She passed a group of neighborhood women gathered outside the bodega, their voices carrying in the cool night air.

Jasmine kept her head down, gripping the cash in her pocket. They didn't know her struggle, didn't know what it was like to fight every day just to keep her kids fed. She had bigger problems.

At home, she counted the money under the dim kitchen light. She peeled off three hundred to give to Mr. Collins, enough to hold him off for another week. The rest she stashed in an old coffee can under the sink, where no one would think to look.

Her kids slept peacefully on the couch, unaware of the risks she'd just taken for them. Jasmine sank onto the mattress in the corner, her body heavy with exhaustion but her mind racing.

The rush of adrenaline from earlier still lingered, a dangerous kind of high that whispered in her ear. If she could pull off one more hit, maybe she could get ahead, pay off the rest of the rent, buy Christmas gifts for her babies.

But the thought of getting caught, of losing everything, made her stomach twist. She had to be smart. Careful. This wasn't a game.

Jasmine stared at the ceiling, the sounds of the streets outside lulling her into a restless sleep.

Tomorrow, she'd decide if the hustle was worth the risk.

When Jasmine woke up the next day Jasmine wasn't the same scared woman who swiped her first bag. She felt she was founding her rhythm, her flow. The streets might chew some people up, but not her. She had to learn the art of boosting fast: know the cameras, spot the blind spots, and always act like you belong.

The first thing she did was switch up her look. The hoodies were gone, replaced with tight jeans, sleek ponytails, and makeup that screamed "I got money." If she was gonna hit these high-end stores, she had to look like the type who belonged there. A little bit of lipstick and fake confidence went a long way.

Jasmine would make her moves at night when the malls were quieter, the rich folks long gone, and the clerks too tired to notice much. She scoped out her spots during the day, watching who worked where, which sections were busiest, and which had the loosest security. Louis Vuitton, Chanel, Gucci those were goldmines. She'd pick her targets, move smooth, and get out before anyone knew what hit 'em.

Tonight was no different. She strutted into the mall, her confidence on full display. The clicks of her heels echoed in the halls as she entered her mark: a high-end shoe store that sold heels worth more than her monthly rent. She didn't waste time. Her sharp eyes zeroed in on a pair of Jimmy Choos, tags glittering with their $1,500 price.

The trick was in the details. Jasmine had learned to cut the security tags with a small pair of scissors she hid in her bra. With a smooth motion, she snipped the tag, slipped the heels into a shopping bag from another store, and headed for the exit like she owned the place.

Outside, the adrenaline hit her like a drug. Her heart pounded, her blood rushed, but she didn't smile. Not yet. The game wasn't over 'til she was out of the parking lot.

In the neighborhood, the gossip was getting loud. The block always had its talkers, and Jasmine's sudden glow-up had them chirping like crows on a wire.

"I saw her with a new weave ponytail, inches touchin' her ass," one woman said on her stoop, lighting a cigarette.

"Probably trickin'. Ain't no way them two jobs she got coverin' all that."

Jasmine didn't care. Let 'em talk. They didn't know her hustle or what she was going through. They didn't know what it took to keep her kids fed and her lights on. As long as her babies had what they needed, the block could keep her name in their mouths.

It wasn't long before her moves started paying off in a bigger way. Marcus came through again, flipping her goods for quick cash, but Jasmine wasn't satisfied with his cut. Five hundred dollars for a $2,000 bag? Nah, she needed more.

One night, after dropping off a load of designer sneakers, Marcus slid her a card. "This dude, Trey, he pay better. But he don't deal with no bullshit. You mess with him, you better be on your game."

Trey wasn't like Marcus. He wasn't grimy or loud. He was sharp, clean, and professional. His house was in a gated community, the type of place Jasmine only ever saw in magazines. When she met him, he didn't waste time.

"You boostin', huh?" Trey said, sitting back on his plush leather couch. His Rolex sparkled under the chandelier.

Jasmine nodded, her nerves bubbling beneath her calm facade. "Yeah, I'm pretty good at what I do."

He smirked. "Good ain't enough. I need reliable. I need someone who can get me quality shit, no drama, no heat."

"I can do that," Jasmine said firmly.

Trey tested her at first, giving her smaller jobs. She hit a Nordstrom, cleaned out the jewelry section, and brought back three necklaces worth over $10,000. Trey handed her three grand without blinking, and Jasmine knew she was in.

The money was coming in fast now. Jasmine paid off her rent, bought her kids new coats, and even treated herself to a trip to the nail salon. But with money came more eyes on her. The neighborhood whispers turned into straight-up accusations.

"She gotta be stealin'," one woman sneered as Jasmine walked past.

"Or she got herself a sugar daddy," another laughed, loud enough for Jasmine to hear.

Jasmine didn't stop. Didn't look back. Let them hate. She wasn't doin' this for them.

The hustle, though, wasn't without its dangers. One night, she hit a Saks Fifth Avenue and got a little too greedy. She grabbed a coat, a bag, and a pair of earrings, stuffing them all into her bag. On her way out, she noticed a security guard eyeing her. Her heart froze. She felt his stare burning into her back as she walked toward the door.

Stay calm. Stay cool.

The second she stepped outside, she bolted, heels clicking against the pavement as she ran to her car. Her hands shook as she started the engine and peeled out of the parking lot. She didn't relax until she was miles away, parked in a dark alley, clutching the wheel with white knuckles.

"Damn," she whispered, exhaling. "That was too close."

She knew she had to tighten up. The streets were unforgiving, and one mistake could cost her everything.

Her connection with Trey grew stronger, and he started putting her onto bigger deals. He introduced her to other buyers who specialized in flipping high-end goods to overseas markets. The pay was better, but the stakes were higher. These weren't Marcus's type of people; they were serious players, the kind who didn't tolerate screw-ups.

Jasmine found herself walking a fine line. She was good at what she did, no doubt. But the deeper she got into the game, the more she realized how dangerous it was. One wrong move, and she could end up in jail or worse.

. . . .

LATE ONE NIGHT, JASMINE sat in her apartment counting a stack of bills. The kids were asleep, their soft breaths filling the silence. She stared at the money, the adrenaline from her latest score still buzzing in her veins. For the first time in a long time, she felt powerful. Like she was in control.

But deep down, she knew the streets didn't play fair. The game always came with a price. And she was just waiting for the day it came to collect.

As she tucked the money away, a knock sounded at the door. Her heart jumped. It was too late for visitors, and no one ever knocked at her place unless it was bad news.

She grabbed a knife from the counter and approached the door cautiously.

"Who is it?" she called out, her voice steady despite the fear creeping up her spine.

Silence.

Jasmine's grip tightened on the knife as she cracked the door open, just enough to see who it was.

Her blood ran cold.

It was Marcus, but something about his face wasn't right. His usual smirk was gone, replaced by a grim expression.

"Jas, we gotta talk," he said, his voice low. "Shit just got real."

Jasmine stared at him, her gut twisting. She didn't know what he was about to say, but she knew it wasn't good.

Chapter 4: Game Recognize Game

Dwayne sat in his dingy little office tucked in the back of the mall, nursing a lukewarm coffee and his bitterness. The hum of the security cameras filled the silence, and he leaned back in his chair, letting out a long sigh. He used to wear a badge, used to be somebody. Now? He was stuck watching teenagers steal sneakers and middle-aged women shove lipsticks into their purses. His gun was gone, his respect gone, and his pride? Long gone.

It had all gone to hell after that damn sting five years ago. He'd been so close to nailing a crew of professional boosters real criminals but one of his own had snitched him out. Internal Affairs stripped his badge, and he'd been spiraling ever since. The badge meant everything to Dwayne, and without it, he was nothing. Every night he dreamed of getting his revenge, of proving he still had it. That's why he took this shitty mall security job to stay in the game, even if it was at the lowest level.

It started like any other shift: hours of watching bored mall employees and oblivious shoppers on the screens. But then, something caught his eye a woman with a sharp stride, moving through the high-end stores like she belonged there. Most of the thieves he dealt with were sloppy, amateurs. But this woman? She was different. Smooth. Confident. Calculated.

Dwayne zoomed in on the camera feed, following her movements as she slid through racks of expensive clothes at Nordstrom. She picked up a handbag, pretended to examine it, then casually slipped it into a shopping bag she already carried. Her hands were steady, her movements fluid. She was good. Too good.

"Gotcha," Dwayne muttered to himself, a smirk tugging at the corners of his mouth.

He watched as she walked out, her pace steady, her head high. No hesitation, no looking back. The cameras caught every move, but there was no alarm, no employee running after her. She disappeared into the parking lot like a ghost.

Dwayne replayed the footage, his eyes narrowing. She wasn't just lucky this wasn't her first time.

The obsession started that night. He ran her face through the mall's system, matching it to footage from previous weeks. She had hit at least three other stores, always walking out with designer goods and never once getting caught. Her technique was flawless. Dwayne hadn't seen a hustle like this since his cop days, and it lit a fire in him.

"She think she slick," he muttered, pacing his office. "Nah, not on my watch."

He started tracking her movements. Every time she came to the mall, he was watching. He noted the stores she targeted, the times she arrived, the way she scoped out her marks before making her move. She had a pattern, and Dwayne was piecing it together.

Jasmine was completely unaware of the shadow following her. She moved through the mall like it was her playground, her confidence growing with every successful hit. She'd perfected her disguise: sleek ponytail, designer knockoffs, a fake smile that put employees at ease. She didn't see the man watching her from the shadows, didn't feel the weight of his gaze every time she stepped into a store.

Dwayne wasn't just watching, though. He was planning. He wanted more than just to catch her he wanted to destroy her. She was a symbol of everything he hated: people who got away with it, who slipped through the cracks while his own life crumbled.

One night, Dwayne followed her into the parking lot. He stayed far enough back to avoid suspicion, watching as she loaded her latest haul into the trunk of a beat-up sedan. He noted the license plate, running it through his contacts from his old life. Within a few hours, he had her name, her address, even her kids' names.

"Jasmine Carter," he muttered, leaning back in his chair. "We gon' see how long you keep this up."

He started digging into her life, learning everything he could. Single mom, two jobs, evictions, her story was one he'd seen a hundred times before. But he didn't feel pity. All he saw was an opportunity. She was desperate, and desperate people made mistakes. He just had to wait for her to slip up.

The first move was subtle. Dwayne left an anonymous tip with mall management, suggesting they tighten security in the high-end stores. He knew it wouldn't stop Jasmine, but it might make her nervous. And nervous people got sloppy.

Sure enough, her next hit didn't go as smoothly. The store had added new cameras, and Jasmine hesitated for a moment before making her move. Dwayne watched it all unfold on the screens, a grin spreading across his face. She still got away, but he could see the tension in her shoulders as she walked out.

"She feelin' the heat now," he muttered, leaning back with satisfaction.

But Dwayne wasn't just satisfied with watching. He wanted to make it personal. He started leaving little messages for Jasmine just enough to let her know someone was onto her. A folded piece of paper tucked under her windshield wiper: *"Careful, girl. Eyes everywhere."* A random man stopping her in the mall parking lot to ask if she "lost something," then walking away before she could answer.

At first, Jasmine brushed it off as paranoia. But the notes kept coming, the strange encounters piling up. She started looking over her shoulder, her once-steady confidence starting to waver.

Dwayne could feel her unraveling, and he fed off it. He was in control now, pulling the strings. But he didn't want her to quit he wanted to catch her in the act, to make her fall so hard she'd never get back up. He wanted her to feel the humiliation he'd felt when he lost his badge, the hopelessness that came with knowing your life was over.

He spent nights sitting in his office, poring over footage, piecing together her entire operation. He even reached out to a few old contacts, planting seeds.

Then came the night he decided to make his move. Jasmine had just hit the Louis Vuitton store, walking out with a haul worth thousands. Dwayne was ready. He followed her into the parking lot, staying just far enough behind to avoid being noticed.

But something unexpected happened. As Jasmine loaded the bags into her trunk, she froze. Her head snapped up, her eyes scanning the lot. For a moment, their eyes met across the rows of cars.

Dwayne didn't move. He just smirked, tipping his head slightly like a hunter taunting his prey.

Jasmine's face hardened, and she slammed the trunk shut, climbing into her car and speeding off.

Dwayne stood there, his heart pounding with adrenaline. The game had officially begun.

"Run all you want," he muttered, lighting a cigarette. "I'll still catch you."

Jasmine didn't know it yet, but her every move was now a part of his plan. The trap was set, and Dwayne was ready to watch her fall.

Chapter 5: Keepin' It Lowkey

Jasmine sat on the edge of her bed, the stack of cash spread out in front of her like a deck of cards. The rent was paid, the lights were back on, and Christmas presents were hidden in the back of her closet, waiting for her kids to wake up to a miracle. But it wasn't relief she felt it was pressure, the kind that sat heavy on her chest like a weight she couldn't shake.

The streets were already talking, and that was the last thing she needed. She could feel it in the way people stared a second too long when she walked by, the hushed conversations that stopped whenever she turned the corner. She knew the gossip was building, and she couldn't let it slip that her "come-up" wasn't exactly on the up-and-up.

Her grandmother, Ms. Gladys, who was visiting the kids for the holidays had been the first to ask. Jasmine was sitting at the table, when the old woman shuffled in with her cane.

"You got some money all the sudden," Ms. Gladys said, her voice sharp despite her years. "Where it come from?"

Jasmine froze, "I been workin' harder, that's all," she said quickly, not looking up. "Picked up some extra shifts."

Ms. Gladys snorted, easing herself into the chair across from her at the kitchen table. "Extra shifts don't pay for no Gucci bag I seen in yo' closet. And I ain't blind I know them kids got more gifts under that tree than you could afford last year."

Jasmine clenched her jaw, willing herself to stay calm. "Don't worry about it, Granny. I got it handled."

"Handled, huh?" Ms. Gladys narrowed her eyes, the weight of her stare heavy. "Don't let me find out you doin' somethin' stupid, Jasmine. These streets don't love nobody, and they damn sure don't love no black woman."

Jasmine swallowed hard, biting back the urge to snap. She respected her grandmother too much for that. "I ain't stupid," she said finally, getting up and walking to the sink. "I'm doin' what I gotta do."

Her kids, on the other hand, didn't care where the money came from they were just happy to finally have things other kids took for granted. Dre, her oldest, tore through his new sneakers like they were gold, holding them up for his little sister to see.

"Ma, these real Jordans?" he asked, his face lit up with excitement.

Jasmine smiled, ruffling his hair. "Yeah, baby. Real deal."

"You rich now?" Nia, her youngest, asked innocently, her big brown eyes wide.

Jasmine laughed, but it was hollow. "Not rich, baby. Just makin' sure y'all got what you need."

The look in their eyes was worth every risk she'd taken. But as much as she loved seeing them happy, the thought of what could happen if she got caught gnawed at the edges of her mind. She couldn't let her guard down not now, not ever.

The block was a different story. The women on the stoop were always whispering, their eyes cutting to Jasmine every time she walked by. She'd hear snippets of their conversations, their voices laced with jealousy and suspicion.

"She think she better than us now?"

"Where she gettin' all that money from? Ain't no way them two jobs payin' for all that shit."

"Bet she boostin' or trickin'. One or the other."

Jasmine held her head high, ignoring them, but inside, it burned. She didn't owe anyone an explanation. Let them talk. They didn't know the half of it. She was grinding for her kids, not for their approval.

Her next hit was already planned. She'd been scoping out a luxury jewelry store downtown, the kind of place where a single necklace could cover her rent for three months. The security was tighter than what she was used to, but Jasmine had a system now. She'd learned how to blend in, how to time her moves perfectly.

The day before the job, she stood outside the store, watching from across the street. She saw the patterns: when the employees switched shifts, which guards were lazy, where the cameras pointed. She took mental notes, piecing together the puzzle.

This one was big too big to mess up. But Jasmine couldn't shake the feeling that someone was watching her. The hairs on the back of her neck stood up as she turned to scan the street, her eyes darting from face to face. Nothing seemed out of place, but the feeling lingered.

Dwayne was watching.

From a bench a block away, he tracked her every move, a smug grin tugging at his lips. He'd seen her casing the store, her sharp eyes scanning for weaknesses. She was good real good but not good enough to outsmart him.

"She think she slick," he muttered to himself, taking a sip from his coffee. "We'll see."

Dwayne had been building his case for weeks, piecing together her patterns, tracking her hits. He had enough evidence to nail her, but he wasn't ready to pull the trigger yet. He wanted to see her squirm first, to feel the walls closing in.

The night of the job, Jasmine slipped into the store just before closing, dressed in her usual disguise: sleek clothes, minimal makeup, nothing to draw attention. She moved like she belonged, her steps confident, her eyes scanning the room.

The necklace was right where she'd seen it the day before, glittering under the glass. A quick glance told her the clerk was distracted, chatting with a couple at the counter. Perfect.

With a practiced motion, Jasmine slipped the glass case open, her fingers closing around the necklace. She tucked it into her bag and walked out without a second glance, her heart pounding.

But as she stepped into the night, the feeling of being watched came back stronger than ever. She quickened her pace, her eyes scanning the shadows. Was it just her nerves, or was someone really out there?

• • • •

BACK AT HOME, JASMINE tucked the necklace into a drawer, her mind racing. She couldn't shake the feeling that something was off, that she was slipping. The pressure was getting to her, but she couldn't stop now. Not when she'd come this far.

As she sat on the couch, counting the cash she'd made from her last job, her phone buzzed with a text from Trey: **"Nice work. Got more for you soon."**

Jasmine leaned back, her fingers drumming on the armrest. The hustle was paying off, but the stakes were getting higher. She couldn't afford to mess up not now, not ever.

Outside, a car idled in the street, its headlights cutting through the dark. Dwayne sat behind the wheel, his eyes fixed on her apartment. He smirked, lighting a cigarette.

"Game on," he muttered, the smoke curling around his face.

Jasmine didn't know it yet, but her every move was under a microscope. And Dwayne? He was just waiting for the perfect moment to strike.

Dwayne sat in his dimly lit office, staring at the mall's security footage with a cigarette dangling from his lips. His smirk was wicked as he rewound the tape, watching Jasmine's latest move for the tenth time. She was smooth too smooth but he was one step ahead now. He'd spent weeks manipulating the store managers, convincing them that their lackluster security made them easy targets.

"Y'all wanna keep losin' money, or y'all wanna do somethin' about it?" he'd said, leaning on his charm while sitting across from the Louis Vuitton manager. His tone was calm, persuasive, but the edge in his voice made it clear he wasn't just offering suggestions.

By the end of the week, new cameras were installed, extra guards were scheduled, and silent alarms were placed under the counters. Dwayne's trap was set, and Jasmine was walking right into it.

Jasmine wasn't feeling right that night. Something about the air felt heavy, like the streets were whispering warnings she couldn't quite hear. But she shook it off, pulling her hair into a sleek bun and slipping into her knockoff designer coat. The kids were tucked in, and the rent was due again. She had no time for paranoia.

Tonight, she planned to hit the jewelry counter at Nordstrom. She'd been scoping it for days saw the lazy clerks, the blind spots, and the piece she wanted: a diamond bracelet that could net her $2,000 easy. Quick grab, quick flip, and she'd be good for the month.

The mall was busy, packed with last-minute holiday shoppers, which worked in her favor. Nobody paid attention to a woman casually strolling through, looking like she had money to burn. She smiled politely at the clerk, pretending to admire a necklace while her eyes darted to the bracelet.

"You need help with somethin'?" the clerk asked, her tone indifferent, already distracted by another customer.

"Nah, just browsin'," Jasmine said, flashing a practiced smile.

Her fingers itched as she timed her move. The clerk turned away, bending to grab a box from behind the counter, and Jasmine made her move. She slipped the bracelet into her bag with one fluid motion, her heart pounding but her face calm.

She started toward the exit, her steps steady. But then

BEEP! BEEP! BEEP!

The alarms screamed, slicing through the air like sirens in the night. Jasmine froze for half a second, her stomach dropping. Panic surged through her veins, but she forced herself to keep walking, her face a mask of indifference.

"Ma'am! Excuse me!" a security guard shouted, his voice cutting through the chaos.

Jasmine's brain went into overdrive. She sped up, weaving through the crowd, her breathing sharp and shallow. The guard was closing in, but she couldn't look back. Not now.

She hit the door running, the cold night air slapping her face as she sprinted toward the parking lot. Her lungs burned, her legs ached, but she didn't stop until she reached her car. She jumped in, slamming the door behind her and peeling out of the lot without a second thought.

Her hands shook as she gripped the wheel, her knuckles white. She glanced at the rearview mirror, half expecting flashing lights or a guard chasing her down, but the lot was quiet. She let out a shaky breath, her chest heaving.

"That was too close," she muttered, wiping sweat from her brow.

Dwayne watched the footage later, his smirk widening as he replayed the moment the alarms went off. He could almost feel her panic through the screen, see the way her confidence cracked for just a second. It wasn't enough to catch her, not yet. But it was enough to let her know someone was watching.

"She ain't untouchable," he said to himself, snuffing out his cigarette. "She gon' slip."

Jasmine sat at her kitchen table, the bracelet lying in front of her like a curse. The kids were asleep, and the apartment was too quiet, the weight of what had just happened pressing down on her. She couldn't shake the feeling that this wasn't random, that the alarms going off wasn't just bad luck.

She thought about the past few weeks the strange notes, the lingering feeling of being watched. It didn't add up. Somebody was onto her, but who?

The streets were talkin', but they always did. Could it be one of her buyers? A hater from the block? Her thoughts raced, each possibility worse than the last.

Her phone buzzed, snapping her out of her spiral. It was Trey, her high-end buyer.

"Yo, you got what I asked for?" his text read.

Jasmine stared at the message for a long moment before replying. "Yeah. Meet same spot tomorrow."

The next day, Jasmine met Trey in an abandoned warehouse on the outskirts of town. It was their usual spot, quiet and out of the way. She handed him the bracelet, her hands still trembling slightly.

"You aight?" Trey asked, eyeing her. "You look shook."

"I'm good," she said quickly, forcing a smile. "Just a long night."

He didn't press, just handed her the cash and nodded. But as she walked back to her car, Jasmine couldn't shake the feeling that her world was closing in.

Back at the mall, Dwayne was putting the final pieces of his plan into motion. He'd already manipulated the store managers into adding more security, but now he was going straight to the mall's corporate office. He painted a picture of a sophisticated shoplifting ring, a crew hitting stores with surgical precision.

"They don't care about alarms," he told them, his voice full of urgency. "They know the gaps in your system. If you don't tighten up, you're gonna lose a lot more than you already have."

They bought it, of course. Dwayne's years as a cop gave him an air of authority that was hard to argue with. By the time he left the meeting, the mall was rolling out new measures: plainclothes security, upgraded cameras, and stricter protocols.

Jasmine didn't know any of this as she planned her next move. She only knew that the pressure was building, the risks growing. She sat in her car outside the mall, her hands gripping the wheel as she tried to steady her breathing.

"You can't stop now," she told herself, her voice shaky. "You just gotta be smarter. Careful."

But deep down, she knew the game was changing. The streets were watching, the alarms were louder, and the shadows felt closer. Someone was playing her, setting her up, and she had no idea who.

As she stepped out of the car and headed toward the mall, her heart pounded with a mix of fear and determination. She wasn't going to stop she couldn't. Not until she figured out who was behind this, and not until she got ahead.

Dwayne watched from his usual spot, his eyes sharp as they tracked her every move. The game was in full swing now, and he was just waiting for the moment she made a mistake.

"Let's see how slick you really are," he muttered, a twisted smile spreading across his face.

Jasmine didn't know it yet, but the next move would decide everything.

Jasmine leaned against the cracked countertop in her kitchen, counting out a thick stack of twenties with trembling fingers. The hustle was hitting harder than ever, and the money was coming in fast. She had paid up the rent two months in advance, stocked the fridge with real food, and her kids' Christmas tree glowed with more presents than she could've dreamed. But it wasn't enough. It was never enough.

Her phone buzzed on the counter. She glanced down: a text from Sharice.

"We hittin' that Neiman Marcus tomorrow or what? Need that bread, girl."

Jasmine hesitated before replying. Recruiting Sharice and Dani had been a gamble. She'd always run solo, trusting no one, but the stores were getting sharper, and the jobs were getting bigger. She needed backup to make the moves she wanted. Sharice and Dani had seemed like a good fit: Sharice was flashy, good at keeping attention on herself, while Dani was quiet, slick with her hands. But now? Jasmine wasn't so sure.

She shot back a quick reply: **"Yeah. Be ready at 8. No games."**

The next morning, Jasmine met the girls at a parking lot a few blocks from the mall. Sharice was already there, leaning against her car in a skintight dress and six-inch heels, her long red weave catching the morning light.

"Girl, you lookin' like a damn Christmas ornament," Jasmine snapped, stepping out of her car. "You tryna steal or get chose?"

"Please, Jas," Sharice shot back, blowing a bubble with her gum. "Ain't nobody payin' me no mind when I look this good. They think I'm here to shop."

Jasmine rolled her eyes as Dani pulled up, stepping out of her car in a plain hoodie and jeans, her face bare. Dani didn't say much, just nodded and slid her hands into her pockets. Jasmine appreciated that about her Dani wasn't here for the drama. She was here to get the job done.

Inside the mall, the plan was simple: Sharice would distract the clerks while Jasmine and Dani made the grabs. Jasmine had already scoped the store, knew exactly what racks to hit, and where the cameras couldn't see.

As they moved through the aisles, Sharice turned on her charm, chatting loudly with a clerk, pulling dresses off racks, and holding them up to the light.

"Girl, this one would look fire on me," Sharice said, her voice carrying across the room.

"Ma'am, we don't allow phones in the fitting rooms," the clerk replied, clearly flustered by Sharice's loud energy.

While Sharice kept the attention on her, Jasmine and Dani moved swiftly. Jasmine grabbed three leather handbags, slipping them into a shopping bag Dani held open. Dani moved like a ghost, her fingers grazing a pair of sunglasses and a scarf before they disappeared into the bag.

"Got it," Dani whispered, her voice low as they maneuvered toward the exit.

But Sharice wasn't done. As Jasmine and Dani slipped out the door, Sharice kept chatting with the clerk, twirling her hair and giggling. By the time she finally strolled out, Jasmine was fuming.

"Sharice, what the hell was that?" Jasmine hissed as they piled into the car.

"Chill, Jas," Sharice replied, popping her gum. "I was playin' my part."

"You playin' too damn much. This ain't a joke."

Sharice waved her off, pulling out her phone to snap a selfie. "Whatever. We good. Nobody even looked at y'all."

The job was a success, but it didn't take long for the cracks to show. Later that night, Jasmine heard the buzz. Word on the block was that Sharice had been bragging about the score to anyone who'd listen.

"She out here talkin' 'bout Neiman Marcus like it's a damn payday loan," one woman said to Jasmine, her tone laced with envy. "You better watch her."

Jasmine clenched her jaw. She didn't need loose lips blowing up their spot. She confronted Sharice the next day, catching her outside her building.

"Why the hell you out here talkin' 'bout the hustle?" Jasmine barked, her voice low but sharp.

"I ain't say nothin' serious," Sharice said, rolling her eyes. "Just lettin' folks know we up. What's the big deal?"

"The big deal is you gon' get us caught, Sharice!" Jasmine snapped. "Keep yo' mouth shut, or you out."

Sharice scoffed but didn't argue, though Jasmine could see the defiance in her eyes.

The gossip wasn't the only problem. Rival boosters were sniffing around, drawn by the noise Sharice had stirred up. Jasmine noticed new faces in her usual spots, slick women with sharp eyes and quick hands, working the same stores she had marked as her territory.

At first, Jasmine let it slide. There was enough money to go around. But when she caught one of them, a tall woman with short blond hair, eyeing a bag she'd been planning to grab, Jasmine couldn't stay quiet.

"Yo, back off," Jasmine said, stepping in front of the rack. "This mine."

"Yours?" Blondie replied with a smirk. "Ain't no names on it, sweetheart."

Jasmine didn't flinch. "You don't wanna do this."

Blondie stared her down for a moment before backing off with a laugh. But Jasmine knew it wasn't over.

The heat was rising. The jobs were getting riskier, the stakes higher. Jasmine started watching her back, feeling the paranoia creep in. She didn't trust Sharice, didn't trust the streets. Dani was the only one she could count on, but even then, Jasmine kept her distance. Trusting anyone too much was a weakness she couldn't afford.

• • • •

ONE NIGHT, AFTER A successful job, Jasmine sat in her car, counting the cash Trey had handed her for the haul. The streets were quiet, the air heavy. She couldn't shake the feeling that something was coming, that the hustle was closing in on her.

Her phone buzzed with a text from Sharice: **"We hittin' Saks tomorrow? Got my eye on somethin' special."**

Jasmine stared at the message for a long moment before replying: **"Not tomorrow. Lay low for a bit."**

She needed time to think, to figure out her next move. The game was getting too crowded, too loud. And Jasmine wasn't about to let anyone take her down.

Outside her apartment, a car idled in the shadows. Dwayne sat behind the wheel, watching as Jasmine got out of her car, her bags in hand. His eyes were cold, calculating.

"She in too deep now," he muttered, lighting a cigarette. "Just a matter of time."

Jasmine didn't notice him as she walked inside, but the feeling of being watched lingered, a chill crawling up her spine. She glanced over her shoulder before shutting the door, locking it tight.

The game was changing, and Jasmine was starting to realize she wasn't the only one playing.

Chapter 8: He Said, She Said

Jasmine walked through the block, head high, her steps confident. The streets were buzzing, but the energy wasn't all good. Her name had been on too many lips lately, and she could feel the weight of every glance, every whisper. She knew the drill when you start winning, people start watching. And when people watch too hard, they get messy.

She ducked into the corner store to grab some smokes, her nerves eating at her. The cashier, a nosy old man everyone called Mr. Clarence, leaned over the counter as she paid.

"You out here makin' moves, huh, Jasmine?" he said, his voice laced with something between curiosity and jealousy.

Jasmine shot him a look. "I'm just tryin' to live, Mr. Clarence. Why everybody actin' like they know my business?"

He chuckled, shaking his head. "Ain't nobody gotta know it, girl. The streets talkin' for you."

When she stepped back outside, the air felt heavier, the gossip thicker. A group of women sat on the stoop, their voices low but loud enough for Jasmine to hear as she walked past.

"Who she think she is, walkin' round here like she a super model?" one said.

"I heard she stealin' other folks' hustle," another chimed in. "Bet she don't even got the guts to do it herself. Prob'ly sendin' them lil' girls she hang with."

Jasmine stopped in her tracks, turning slowly toward the group. Her eyes locked on the loudest one Keisha, a mouthy chick who always had something to say. Keisha smirked, her arms folded, daring Jasmine to respond.

"What you say, Keisha?" Jasmine asked, her tone cold.

Keisha stood, her smirk widening. "I said what I said. You out here thinkin' you run shit, but you ain't the only one tryna eat. You stealin' from people who been doin' this longer than you."

Jasmine took a step closer, her fists clenched at her sides. "Ain't nobody stealin' nothin'. You mad 'cause I'm doin' better than you? Stay mad."

The stoop erupted in gasps and laughter, Keisha's girls hyping her up. But Keisha wasn't laughing. She stepped forward, her face inches from Jasmine's.

"Better watch yourself, Jas. These streets don't like a thief," she hissed.

Jasmine didn't flinch. "And I don't like a hater."

By the time Jasmine got home, her blood was boiling. She slammed the door shut, pacing the small apartment as she tried to calm down. Her phone buzzed on the table, pulling her from her thoughts. It was Dani.

"You hearin' this mess?" Dani said as soon as Jasmine answered.

"I just ran into it. Keisha runnin' her mouth like she got a death wish."

"She tellin' everybody you stole her man's side hustle. Sayin' you snatched her plug."

Jasmine rolled her eyes. "Her man ain't got nothin' I need. She mad I'm better at this than she ever was."

"Well, watch your back," Dani warned. "Keisha don't just talk. She cut throat."

"Let her bring it," Jasmine snapped, ending the call.

Meanwhile, Dwayne was playing a different game. He sat in his office, the glow of the security monitors reflecting off his smug grin. He had been keeping tabs on Jasmine's buyers, piecing together her network one deal at a time. When he caught wind of a big drop happening the next day, he knew it was his chance.

"Let's see how she like this," he muttered, picking up his phone.

The call was quick, the details brief. A tip to the cops about a "suspicious operation" at an old warehouse. He didn't need to say much just enough to point them in the right direction.

Jasmine showed up at the warehouse the next evening, a bag of high-end goods in her hand. Trey was already there, leaning against his car with a cigarette between his lips. He didn't look happy.

"You late," he said, flicking the cigarette to the ground.

"Traffic," Jasmine lied, handing him the bag. "It's all there. You got my cut?"

Trey nodded, pulling out an envelope thick with cash. But before Jasmine could grab it, the sound of tires screeching filled the air. Red and blue lights flashed, and sirens wailed as three unmarked cars surrounded them.

"Shit!" Trey yelled, throwing the bag into his car and slamming the door.

Jasmine's heart raced as she bolted for the alley, her feet pounding against the pavement. The cops shouted behind her, their voices sharp and urgent. She ducked behind a dumpster, her chest heaving, her mind racing.

How the hell did they know? she thought, panic tightening her throat.

She stayed hidden as the cops swarmed the warehouse, cuffing Trey and tearing through his car. The envelope of cash was gone, her big payday slipping through her fingers.

When the coast was clear, Jasmine crept out of her hiding spot, her body trembling. Her phone buzzed in her pocket it was Dani again.

"Jas, you good?" Dani asked, her voice frantic.

"No," Jasmine snapped. "The drop got raided. Trey's done."

Dani cursed under her breath. "How the hell they know?"

"I don't know, but somebody set this up," Jasmine growled. "And when I find out who, they gon' pay."

Back at his office, Dwayne watched the live news report on his laptop. Footage of Trey being led away in handcuffs played on the screen, and the reporter talked about a "major breakthrough in an organized theft ring." Dwayne leaned back in his chair, satisfied.

"Checkmate," he muttered, lighting a cigarette.

· · · ·

BUT HE WASN'T DONE yet. Jasmine had escaped, and that meant the game was still on. He didn't just want to disrupt her hustle he wanted to break her completely.

Jasmine sat in her car, the adrenaline still coursing through her veins. She stared at the empty passenger seat, where the envelope of cash should've been. Her chest tightened as anger bubbled up inside her.

This was more than bad luck. Somebody was out to get her, and she was determined to figure out who.

As she drove home, her mind raced with possibilities. Keisha? One of her buyers? The streets were full of snakes, and Jasmine knew she couldn't trust anyone.

When she pulled up to her apartment, the shadows seemed darker, the air heavier. She locked the door behind her, her senses on high alert. She didn't know who was coming for her, but one thing was clear: the game was getting dangerous.

And Jasmine wasn't sure how much longer she could keep winning.

Jasmine sat in her car, her fingers tapping on the steering wheel. The streets were quiet this late, but her mind was anything but. She stared at the number Dani had given her, scrawled on the back of a napkin. This could be the break she needed a new plug, someone out of town who didn't know about the heat she was catching on the block.

She dialed the number, her heart pounding as it rang. A deep voice answered on the third ring.

"Who dis?"

"It's Jasmine. Dani said you buy high-end," she replied, trying to sound steady.

There was a pause, then the voice softened slightly. "Aight, Dani cool. What you got?"

"Bags, jewelry, some clothes. All quality."

"I'm listenin'. You local?"

"Atlanta. But I move smart. No bullshit."

The man chuckled. "Smart is good. I don't do sloppy. Meet me tomorrow, 10 p.m. The old gas station off Route 42."

Jasmine hung up, her stomach twisting. She didn't know much about this guy just that he went by the name Black, and he paid double what Trey did. But she needed this. After the raid, her usual buyers were too scared to deal, and her cash flow had dried up. Black was a risk, but one she couldn't afford not to take.

The gas station was a shell of its former self, abandoned and crumbling. Jasmine pulled up, her headlights cutting through the darkness. A black SUV was already parked there, its windows tinted so dark she couldn't see inside.

She grabbed the duffel bag from her trunk, her nerves jangling as she approached. The SUV's door opened, and a tall man stepped out, his frame broad and intimidating. He wore a fitted hoodie and jeans, his face partially hidden by the shadow of the gas station's overhang.

"You Jasmine?" he asked, his voice calm but commanding.

"That's me," she replied, holding up the bag. "You Black?"

He nodded, motioning for her to follow him to the back of the SUV. He opened the trunk, revealing a small table and a scale. Jasmine placed the bag on the table, unzipping it to reveal its contents: two designer handbags, a pair of diamond earrings, and a stack of brand-name clothes.

Black inspected the items carefully, his movements deliberate. He didn't say much, but Jasmine could tell he knew his stuff. When he was done, he nodded.

"Clean work. I like that. You want cash or wire?"

"Cash," Jasmine said quickly.

Black smirked, pulling a stack of bills from a hidden compartment. He counted it out in front of her, the sound of the crisp bills filling the silence.

"That's double what you'd get local," he said, handing her the money. "But lemme tell you somethin'. You got heat on you, don't you?"

Jasmine's stomach flipped. "What makes you say that?"

"I hear things," Black said, his tone steady. "Your name buzzin' too much. That's bad for business. You wanna keep workin' with me, you stay lowkey. No noise, no drama. You draw heat to me, and we done. Understand?"

Jasmine nodded, her grip tightening on the money. "I hear you."

"Good. Now get outta here. I don't like sittin' in one spot too long."

Driving back, Jasmine's mind raced. Black was right her name was ringing out too loud on the block. She needed to tighten up, keep her circle small. Sharice's big mouth had already caused problems, and Keisha's drama wasn't helping. If she wanted to keep getting money, she had to stay invisible.

The cash felt heavy in her lap, a reminder of what was at stake. This was more than just survival now. This was about proving she could play the game better than anyone else.

The next day, Jasmine met with Dani to split the money from the deal. They sat in Jasmine's kitchen, the blinds drawn tight.

"This Black dude legit," Jasmine said, counting out Dani's share. "He payin' double, but he don't play. Told me to keep it quiet."

Dani nodded, her expression serious. "That's smart. Too many people out here talkin'. Sharice been runnin' her mouth again."

Jasmine slammed the stack of bills on the table, her frustration boiling over. "I'm 'bout done with Sharice. She a liability."

"She reckless," Dani agreed. "But she good at what she do. You just gotta keep her in check."

Jasmine sighed, running a hand through her hair. "I can't afford no more mistakes. Not with Black in the picture."

But keeping quiet was easier said than done. By the end of the week, word had already spread about Jasmine's new plug. She caught Keisha whispering with one of the other boosters outside the corner store, their eyes cutting to her as she walked by.

"You hear she workin' with that outta-town dude?" Keisha said loud enough for Jasmine to hear. "Wonder how long that will last?."

Jasmine stopped in her tracks, turning to face Keisha. "You got somethin' to say, Keisha?"

Keisha smirked, leaning against the wall. "Just sayin', you better watch yourself. Shit real out here."

Jasmine stepped closer, her voice low and dangerous. "The streets don't scare me and yo ass don't either!"

The tension crackled between them, but Keisha backed down, her smirk fading. Jasmine turned and walked away, her heart pounding. She couldn't let Keisha or anyone else derail her hustle.

Jasmine's next deal with Black went even smoother. She brought him a bigger haul three handbags, a gold bracelet, and a pair of designer heels and walked away with more money than she'd ever made in one run.

"You good at this," Black said as he handed her the cash. "But remember what I said. No noise."

"I got you," Jasmine replied, stuffing the money into her bag.

But as she drove home, the feeling of being watched crept over her again. She glanced in the rearview mirror, her eyes scanning the road. A black sedan followed her for a few blocks before turning off, but the unease lingered.

Jasmine parked in front of her building, her grip tight on the steering wheel. The streets were quiet, but the shadows felt alive, like they were closing in. She locked the car and hurried inside, double-checking the locks on her door.

As she sat on her couch, counting the money, her phone buzzed with a text from Dani: **"We good for tomorrow?"**

Jasmine stared at the message, her mind racing. She was in deep now, too deep to turn back. The money was good, but the stakes were getting higher, the risks sharper.

She typed a reply: **"Yeah. Let's get it."**

But deep down, Jasmine knew the game was only getting more dangerous. And the shadows weren't just in her head they were real. Someone was watching, waiting for her next move.

Jasmine pulled into her usual spot outside her apartment, cutting the engine and letting the quiet hum of the night settle around her. It had been a long day, and her nerves were shot. The hustle was wearing her down, but the money made it hard to stop. She leaned back in the driver's seat, exhaling deeply, when something caught her eye. A folded piece of paper stuck under her windshield wiper.

Her chest tightened. She glanced around the lot, the shadows stretching long and dark. The streetlight overhead flickered, casting a dim, uneven glow. Nobody was around at least not that she could see.

"What the hell?" she muttered, stepping out of the car and snatching the note. She unfolded it, her stomach twisting as she read the scrawled handwriting:

"Watch yourself. Eyes everywhere."

Her pulse quickened. The note was short, simple, but it hit like a punch to the gut. She crumpled it in her hand, looking around the lot again, but there was nothing. Just the faint sound of distant sirens and the hum of passing cars.

"Somebody playin' games," she said under her breath, her voice trembling.

Jasmine hurried inside, locking the door behind her. She double-checked the locks, her heart racing. Whoever left the note knew something, and that meant she wasn't as invisible as she thought.

The next day, she couldn't shake the feeling that she was being watched. At the mall, while scoping out a new store, she caught herself glancing over her shoulder every few minutes. She tried to focus, her eyes scanning the layout, but the paranoia was relentless.

As she moved toward the exit, a man in a security uniform crossed her path, and her breath hitched. He didn't look at her, didn't do anything unusual, but the sight of him sent a jolt of fear through her. She quickened her pace, her hands gripping the shopping bag tightly.

In the parking lot, she checked her car before getting in, her eyes darting to every corner of the lot. Nothing seemed out of place, but her gut told her otherwise.

Later that night, another note appeared.

"You can't run forever."

Jasmine's hands shook as she read it. She threw the note onto the passenger seat, her mind racing. She locked the doors and looked around.

She called Dani as soon as she got home, her voice shaky. "Dani, somebody messin' with me."

"What you mean?" Dani asked, her tone sharp.

"Somebody leavin' notes on my car. Talkin' 'bout 'watch yourself' and all that. I think somebody followin' me."

"Shit, Jas. You think it's Keisha?"

"I don't know," Jasmine said, pacing her living room. "But this don't feel right. This feel crazy."

"Maybe it's time to chill for a bit," Dani suggested. "Lay low, see if it blow over."

Jasmine shook her head, even though Dani couldn't see her. "I can't stop now. I'm too deep in this. But I gotta find out who doin' this."

Unbeknownst to Jasmine, Dwayne was watching. He'd been watching for weeks. Sitting in his car a few blocks away, he grinned as he saw her silhouette pacing through the window. The notes were doing their job, getting under her skin, making her second-guess herself. She felt she was slipping, and he loved every second of it.

"Paranoia's a bitch, ain't it?" he muttered, lighting a cigarette.

He knew how to play the long game. It wasn't enough to catch her he wanted to break her, make her unravel until she fell into his hands. Every note, every shadow she thought she saw, was another thread he pulled loose.

Jasmine started changing her routine, taking different routes, checking her mirrors constantly. She avoided the usual spots, but the feeling of being followed never left. Every shadow seemed to move, every sound felt like it was meant for her.

One night, she sat in her car outside her apartment, too afraid to go inside. Her phone buzzed, a text from Sharice.

"You good, girl? Ain't seen you 'round."

Jasmine stared at the screen for a long moment before typing back.

"Just busy. Stay outta trouble."

But trouble wasn't something Jasmine could avoid. As she stepped out of the car, she spotted a black sedan parked across the street. Its engine idled softly, the lights off. Her heart pounded as she walked quickly to her door, her keys fumbling in her hand. She glanced back, but the car didn't move.

Once inside, she locked the door and leaned against it, her breathing shallow. She peered through the blinds, but the sedan was gone. Still, the fear lingered.

The final straw came two nights later. Another note, this time taped to her front door.

"Time's up."

Jasmine froze, her breath catching in her throat. She ripped the note down, her hands trembling as she scanned the street. It was empty, but she knew better now. Somebody was out there, and they weren't going away.

She called Dani again, her voice frantic. "Dani, I'm losin' it. They left a note on my door this time."

"Damn, Jas. You think it's the cops?"

"I don't know! I don't know nothin' no more," Jasmine snapped, her voice cracking. "But whoever it is, they want me to know they watchin'."

Dani sighed on the other end of the line. "Maybe it's time to get outta town for a bit. Clear your head."

"Get outta town?" Jasmine barked. "This hustle all I got."

"Then you better figure out how to make it work," Dani said, her tone cold. "Before it's too late."

Jasmine hung up, her chest tight. She didn't know who was behind the notes, but she wasn't about to let them take her down. Not without a fight.

Meanwhile, Dwayne sat in his car, watching the lights in Jasmine's apartment flicker on and off. He could see her shadow moving through the blinds, pacing like a trapped animal. He chuckled to himself, the satisfaction burning brighter than the cigarette in his hand.

"She think she slick," he muttered. "But I'm right here."

The game was far from over, but Dwayne was patient. He knew it was only a matter of time before Jasmine slipped. And when she did, he'd be waiting.

Jasmine didn't know it yet, but the walls were closing in. The pressure was mounting, and shit was getting darker. The question wasn't if she'd fall it was when.

Sharice strutted through the parking lot of the mall, her red-bottom heels clicking on the pavement. She carried herself like she owned the place, a smirk plastered across her face. The money had been coming in steady, and she loved the attention it brought. But what Sharice didn't know was that someone else had been watching her, waiting for the perfect moment to pounce.

Dwayne sat in his car, eyes locked on Sharice as she walked toward her car. He had been following her for days, piecing together her connection to Jasmine. He wasn't sure at first, but after watching them work a few hits together, he knew Sharice was a weak link.

"Gotcha," he muttered, stepping out of his car and adjusting his jacket.

As Sharice reached her car, she fumbled with her keys, too busy scrolling through her phone to notice Dwayne approaching. By the time she looked up, he was standing right in front of her.

"Yo, who the hell" she started, but Dwayne cut her off.

"Relax, Sharice," he said, his tone calm but sharp. "We just need to talk."

Sharice's eyes narrowed as she sized him up. "I don't know you, and I damn sure ain't got nothin' to talk about."

"Oh, you know me now," Dwayne said, flashing his old badge, a relic of his cop days. It wasn't active, but it still carried weight. "And I know you. You rollin' with Jasmine, right?"

Sharice froze, her bravado cracking for a split second before she scoffed. "I don't know no Jasmine."

Dwayne smirked, leaning in close. "Don't play me, girl. I've been watchin'. I know y'all been hittin' these stores, movin' product. And I know you ain't slick enough to be the mastermind. So here's the deal: you help me take her down, or I make sure you go down with her."

Sharice's mouth opened, then shut. Her mind raced as she tried to figure out her next move. "Man, you bluffin'. You ain't got nothin' on me."

Dwayne chuckled, stepping back and pulling out his phone. He swiped through a series of photos Sharice walking into stores with Jasmine, carrying bags out, and meeting buyers. He held the screen up for her to see.

"Bluffin'? Looks pretty solid to me," he said, his tone laced with menace. "Now, you wanna end up in cuffs, or you wanna work with me? 'Cause trust me, sweetheart, the cops won't care about your excuses."

Sharice's stomach sank. She glanced around the lot, her mind screaming for a way out. But the photos were damning, and Dwayne's cold stare told her he wasn't playing.

"What you want?" she finally said, her voice low.

Dwayne smiled, knowing he'd won. "Simple. You keep doin' what you do, but you tell me everything. Where y'all goin', what y'all takin', who you sellin' to. You help me, I keep you outta jail. But you cross me? You goin' down harder than Jasmine."

Sharice hesitated, the weight of the decision pressing down on her. She hated the idea of turning on Jasmine, but the thought of handcuffs and jail cells scared her more.

"Aight," she said through gritted teeth. "I'll tell you what you wanna know."

The first time Sharice fed Dwayne info, she felt sick to her stomach. Jasmine was planning a hit at a high-end boutique downtown, and Sharice tipped Dwayne off about the time and the target. She told herself it was just a one-time thing, a way to buy herself some time, but deep down, she knew she was in too deep.

Jasmine had no idea. She thought Sharice was just being her usual flashy self, running her mouth a little too much but still loyal. The job went off without a hitch, but Jasmine couldn't shake the feeling that something was off. The store had added new cameras and extra staff, almost like they knew she was coming.

"You notice anything weird about that spot?" Jasmine asked Sharice later that night as they counted the cash.

"Weird? Nah, it was smooth," Sharice said, avoiding Jasmine's eyes.

Jasmine frowned but didn't press. She had bigger things to worry about, like moving the next batch of goods.

Dwayne, meanwhile, was thrilled. The info Sharice gave him was solid, and he was building a case against Jasmine piece by piece. But he wasn't satisfied yet. He wanted more. He cornered Sharice in the same parking lot a week later, his demeanor colder than before.

"You did good last time," he said, his voice low. "But I need more. Big scores. High-value targets. And I need names."

Sharice glared at him, her resentment bubbling to the surface. "I ain't givin' you no names. That wasn't the deal."

Dwayne stepped closer, his voice dropping to a menacing whisper. "The deal is whatever I say it is. You think you got choices here? 'Cause I can end this real quick if you want."

Sharice's fists clenched, but she knew better than to push him. "Fine," she muttered. "I'll give you what you need."

Over the next few weeks, Sharice fed Dwayne more details Jasmine's routes, her buyers, her next hits. Each time, Dwayne used the information to tighten the noose, adding more pressure without tipping his hand.

Jasmine, meanwhile, was starting to feel the heat. She noticed more security at her usual spots, more buyers getting skittish. She couldn't figure out why, but the paranoia was eating at her.

One night, after a particularly close call at a designer shoe store, Jasmine turned to Dani. "You think somebody talkin'?"

Dani raised an eyebrow. "Talkin'? Like who?"

"I don't know," Jasmine said, pacing the room. "But somebody gotta be. Feels like they always one step ahead."

Dani shrugged. "Ain't me. Maybe you just gettin' sloppy."

Jasmine shot her a look. "I don't get sloppy."

The cracks in Jasmine's operation were starting to show, and Dwayne knew it was only a matter of time before everything fell apart. But Sharice was struggling to keep her composure. The guilt of betraying Jasmine was eating at her, and the pressure from Dwayne was relentless.

One night, after a particularly heated exchange with Dwayne, Sharice sat in her car, gripping the steering wheel tightly. She felt trapped, caught between loyalty and self-preservation. She wanted out, but she didn't know how.

Her phone buzzed a text from Jasmine: **"We good for tomorrow?"**

Sharice stared at the message, her heart pounding. She typed a reply: **"Yeah, we good."**

But as she hit send, tears welled up in her eyes. She knew she was crossing lines she couldn't uncross, and the weight of it was crushing her.

Jasmine, oblivious to Sharice's betrayal, was focused on the next job. But the unease in her gut was growing stronger. She didn't know it yet, but the walls were closing in fast, and the person she trusted most was the one holding the hammer.

The cold December air bit at Jasmine's cheeks as she leaned against her car, her breath visible in the dim light of the parking lot. The streets were quiet, almost too quiet, but Jasmine couldn't let her nerves show. This was it the big one. A hit that would set her up for months if she played it right. Christmas Eve was the perfect cover; people were too busy with last-minute shopping to notice someone making moves.

Sharice and Dani sat in the car, waiting for Jasmine to go over the plan one last time. Sharice looked edgy, her leg bouncing as she scrolled through her phone. Dani, as usual, was calm and quiet, her hood pulled up over her braids.

Jasmine tapped on the window, motioning for them to get out. "Aight, listen up," she said, her tone sharp. "This ain't no little grab. We hittin' that jewelry spot downtown. Security tight, so we gotta be tighter."

Dani nodded, her face unreadable. Sharice smirked, trying to mask her unease. "We good, Jas. Ain't nobody gon' see us comin'."

"They betta not," Jasmine said, her eyes narrowing. "You know the layout. Dani, you handle the cases. Sharice, you keep the clerk distracted. I'll handle the cameras and grab the goods."

Sharice hesitated, glancing at Dani before speaking. "You sure this the move, Jas? Feels like we pushin' it."

Jasmine shot her a look that could cut glass. "You scared, stay your ass home. But don't be cryin' when we cashin' out without you."

Sharice clenched her jaw but said nothing. Jasmine didn't have time for doubts or second-guessing. This job was her ticket to staying ahead, and she wasn't about to let anyone screw it up.

Across town, Dwayne sat in his unmarked car, sipping stale coffee as he watched the jewelry store from a distance. His sources Sharice included had given him everything he needed to know. Jasmine thought she was slick, but Dwayne was always one step ahead. He'd spent weeks setting this up, pulling strings to ensure everything was in place.

The sting operation was his chance to finally take her down. He'd tipped off the store manager, who had quietly upgraded the security system and placed plainclothes officers inside the store. Dwayne's plan was simple: let Jasmine and her crew think they were winning, then hit them when they least expected it.

"She ain't gettin' away this time," he muttered, a grim smile spreading across his face.

The jewelry store gleamed under bright lights, the display cases filled with diamonds, gold, and everything that screamed money. Jasmine, dressed in a sleek black coat and boots, walked in first, her demeanor calm and confident. She looked like a regular shopper, her sharp eyes taking in every detail.

Sharice followed close behind, her voice loud and cheerful as she struck up a conversation with the clerk. "Ooh, these earrings nice! You think they match my vibe?" she said, laughing.

The clerk smiled, already charmed by her bubbly personality. "They'd look great on you. We've got a sale going on, too."

While Sharice kept the clerk busy, Dani moved quietly to the far end of the store, her fingers quick as she worked on disabling the locks on the display cases. Jasmine slipped into the back, her heart pounding as she approached the security room. She'd studied the layout for weeks, memorizing every camera angle and blind spot.

She found the panel and quickly disconnected the feed, her hands steady despite the adrenaline surging through her. "Showtime," she whispered, heading back toward the showroom.

Outside, Dwayne watched the scene unfold on his tablet, the live security feed giving him a front-row seat. His jaw clenched as he saw Jasmine disable the cameras, her movements precise and confident.

"She too damn good at this," he muttered. But he wasn't worried. The plainclothes officers were already in position, waiting for his signal.

Jasmine moved fast, scooping necklaces, bracelets, and watches into her bag. Dani worked alongside her, their coordination seamless. Sharice's laughter echoed through the store, keeping the clerk distracted as the haul piled up.

"Yo, we almost done," Jasmine hissed, glancing at Dani. "Grab that last case, then we out."

Dani nodded, her fingers working the lock on a case filled with diamond rings. But as she pulled the drawer open, an alarm blared, the sharp sound cutting through the air like a siren.

"Shit!" Jasmine cursed, her heart racing. She looked toward the front of the store, where the clerk's smile had vanished, replaced by wide-eyed panic.

Sharice froze, her face pale. "Jas, what the hell?"

"We gotta go, now!" Jasmine barked, grabbing the bag and bolting for the exit.

But as they reached the door, two men stepped in front of them, their badges flashing. "Atlanta PD. Don't move," one of them said, his voice firm.

Jasmine's mind raced, her eyes darting to the side door. "Dani, that way!" she yelled, shoving Sharice forward.

The three of them sprinted toward the exit, the cops close behind. Jasmine's chest burned as she ran, her grip tight on the bag of stolen goods. She could hear the shouts, the sound of footsteps pounding behind her, but she didn't look back.

Outside, Dwayne stepped out of his car, watching the chaos unfold with a smug grin. This was the moment he'd been waiting for, the culmination of weeks of planning. He pulled out his radio, barking orders to the officers on the scene.

"Don't let 'em get away," he said, his voice cold.

Jasmine burst out of the side door, the cold air hitting her like a slap. She spotted her car parked across the lot and made a beeline for it, her legs screaming with every step. Sharice and Dani were close behind, their faces etched with fear.

"Keys, Jas! Hurry!" Sharice shouted as they reached the car.

Jasmine fumbled with the keys, her hands shaking. The cops were closing in, their shouts growing louder. She finally unlocked the doors, jumping in and starting the engine.

The tires screeched as she peeled out of the lot, the car swerving onto the main road. Jasmine's heart pounded as she glanced in the rearview mirror, the flashing lights of police cars growing smaller in the distance.

"We good?" Dani asked, her voice shaky.

"For now," Jasmine muttered, gripping the wheel tightly.

But deep down, she knew this wasn't over. The game had changed, and the stakes were higher than ever. Dwayne wasn't just watching anymore he was coming for her.

And Jasmine was running out of time.

The girls had decided to lay low for a minute the word spread like wild fire that Sharice had her hand in what had happened and may have been giving info to the law. Sharice, meanwhile, was holed up in a motel on the other side of town, her nerves shot. She couldn't shake the image of Jasmine's face when the alarm went off, the betrayal written all over it. But what choice did she have? Dwayne had her backed into a corner, and jail wasn't an option.

Her phone buzzed on the nightstand. She hesitated before picking it up, her stomach twisting when she saw the message from Jasmine: **"Where you at? We need to talk."**

Sharice stared at the screen, her thumb hovering over the reply button. She knew she couldn't face Jasmine, not after what she'd done. She tossed the phone onto the bed, her chest tight.

The next day, Jasmine hit the streets, asking questions, putting feelers out. She wasn't subtle about it, and it didn't take long for word to spread that she was looking for Sharice.

At the bodega, an old hustler named Rico leaned against the counter, shaking his head. "You really think she gon' show her face 'round here after that?"

"She better," Jasmine said, her voice hard. "Or I'm gon' make it my mission to find her."

Rico smirked, but there was no humor in it. "Careful, Jas. Sometimes people don't play fair."

"Neither do I," she shot back, storming out of the store.

By nightfall, Jasmine was no closer to finding Sharice, and her frustration was boiling over. She sat in her car, staring at her phone, debating whether to call Dani again. Before she could decide, a knock on the window startled her.

She looked up to see Keisha, of all people, smirking at her. "Heard you lookin' for Sharice."

Jasmine rolled down the window slightly, her eyes narrowing. "What you know?"

Keisha shrugged, leaning closer. "Just that she ain't the only one you need to worry about. Word is, somebody else been watchin' you. Real close."

Jasmine's stomach dropped. "Who?"

Keisha smirked. "That's for you to figure out."

Jasmine opened her mouth to press further, but Keisha was already walking away, her laughter echoing in the cold night air.

Later that night, as Jasmine sat alone in her apartment, the weight of it all pressed down on her. She felt trapped, cornered. The streets were colder than ever, and she couldn't shake the feeling that she was playing a game she couldn't win.

Her phone buzzed again, another message from an unknown number: **"Time's running out."**

Jasmine stared at the screen, her anger turning to resolve. Whoever was coming for her, they'd better be ready. Because Jasmine wasn't going down without a fight.

The game wasn't over yet.

Jasmine stared at the room walls, her head pounding from the weight of it all. The floral wallpaper was peeling at the corners, and the air reeked of bleach and cigarette smoke. It was a far cry from home, but right now, she didn't have the luxury of being picky. The streets were too hot, and her name was on every tongue.

She peered through the blinds, her eyes scanning the parking lot. Nothing. Just a couple of beat-up cars and a stray cat digging through a trash bin. Still, the unease wouldn't leave her. She let the blinds snap shut and paced the small room, her nerves frayed.

"Can't keep livin' like this," she muttered to herself, running a hand through her hair.

Her phone buzzed on the cheap nightstand, the screen lighting up with a message from Dani: **"U good?"**

Jasmine hesitated before typing back: **"I'm layin' low. Don't hit me up unless it's important."**

Jasmine had been off the grid for three days, sticking to rundown motels and avoiding all her usual spots. She couldn't trust nobody not Dani, not Sharice, not even herself. The streets were cold, but they weren't stupid. Word would get around eventually, and when it did, she needed to be gone.

The small bag of stolen goods sat on the table, taunting her. It wasn't much, just a couple of necklaces, a bracelet, and a pair of diamond earrings, but it was all she had left from the job. She needed to offload it fast, but her regular buyers were too risky now. Trey was out of the picture, and Black? He'd made it clear he didn't deal with heat.

That left Jasmine scrambling. She scrolled through her phone, searching for numbers she hadn't used in years. Finally, she landed on one: Rico. He wasn't her first choice hell, he wasn't even her tenth but she didn't have options.

Later that night, Jasmine met Rico in an abandoned parking lot on the west side. The streetlights flickered overhead, casting long shadows on the cracked asphalt. Rico leaned against his car, a rusty Crown Vic, puffing on a cigar. His smirk was as greasy as ever, and Jasmine hated that she had to deal with him.

"Look who crawled outta hidin," Rico said, his voice dripping with amusement. "What you got for me, Jas?"

Jasmine didn't bother with pleasantries. She popped the trunk of her car, pulling out the small duffel bag. "Couple chains, some earrings. Real clean, no scratches."

Rico opened the bag, his thick fingers rummaging through the goods. He whistled low, pulling out a necklace and holding it up to the light. "This nice. Real nice. But, uh, I don't know if it's worth what you think it is."

Jasmine's patience was thin. "Don't play with me, Rico. I know what it's worth."

Rico chuckled, tossing the necklace back into the bag. "I ain't playin'. I'm just sayin'... times is hard. Buyers ain't spendin' like they used to."

"How much?" Jasmine asked, her voice clipped.

Rico rubbed his chin, pretending to think. "Three hundred."

Jasmine's blood boiled. "Three hundred? Are you out your damn mind? That shit worth at least two racks!"

Rico shrugged, his smirk never leaving his face. "Ain't nobody payin' full price for hot goods, Jas. Take it or leave it."

Jasmine clenched her fists, her jaw tight. She needed the money, but the insult stung. Still, she couldn't afford to walk away empty-handed. "Fine," she spat. "But this the last time I deal with your cheap ass."

"Suit yourself," Rico said, handing her a stack of crumpled bills.

Jasmine snatched the money and slammed the trunk shut, her anger simmering as she drove off into the night.

Back at the motel, Jasmine counted the money, the pitiful stack of cash reminding her of how far she'd fallen. She'd risked everything for that heist, and this was all she had to show for it. Her chest tightened as frustration bubbled up inside her.

"This ain't it," she muttered, throwing the money onto the bed.

Her phone buzzed again, another message from Dani: **"Sharice poppin' up in spots she shouldn't. Watch out."**

Jasmine's grip on the phone tightened. Sharice. The name was like poison in her veins. She was the reason everything had gone to hell, and now she was out here moving freely, like she didn't have a target on her back.

Jasmine stared at the message, her mind racing. She couldn't stay in hiding forever. The streets were still talking, and the longer she waited, the more control she lost. But moving too soon could cost her everything.

The next morning, Jasmine stepped out of the motel room, her hood pulled low as she scanned the lot. The air was crisp, the silence unsettling. She slid into her car, the duffel bag still sitting on the passenger seat.

Her phone buzzed with a new message: **"Got somethin' for you. Same spot."**

It was from Rico. Jasmine debated ignoring it, but curiosity got the better of her. She needed a win, no matter how small.

At the meet, Rico leaned against his car, holding up a small envelope. "This here might help you out," he said, tossing it to her.

Jasmine caught it, her eyes narrowing. "What's this?"

"Info. Heard some things about your girl Sharice. Thought you might wanna know."

Jasmine opened the envelope, her eyes scanning the scribbled notes inside. An address, a time, and a name: *Dwayne.*

Her stomach dropped. "Dwayne? Who the hell is that?"

Rico shrugged, lighting another cigar. "Don't know much, but word is he been pullin' strings. Sounds like your kinda problem."

Jasmine's grip on the envelope tightened, her mind reeling. She didn't trust Rico, but the pieces were starting to come together. If Sharice had flipped, it made sense she wasn't working alone.

Back at the motel, Jasmine sat on the edge of the bed, the envelope in her lap. She couldn't shake the feeling that she was walking into a trap, but she didn't have a choice. The game was closing in, and if she didn't act fast, she'd lose everything.

Her phone buzzed again, a new message from an unknown number: **"You're running out of time."**

Jasmine's jaw clenched as she read the words, her anger hardening into resolve. She didn't know who was behind it all, but one thing was clear: she wasn't about to go down without a fight.

The streets were watching, the stakes were rising, and Jasmine was ready to play the game her way.

Jasmine sat in the dim light of the motel room, the air thick with stale cigarette smoke and anger. Her fist clenched around the crumpled note Rico had given her. *Dwayne.* The name burned in her mind like a bad tattoo. She didn't know the man, but she damn sure knew his type. Dirty, controlling, always pulling strings from the shadows. But Sharice? That betrayal cut deep.

Sharice had been her girl, her partner in the hustle. They'd come up together, hit licks together. And now, Sharice had flipped, working with the enemy? Jasmine's blood boiled just thinking about it.

"She gotta pay for this," Jasmine muttered, pacing the small room. Her sneakers scuffed against the worn carpet, her mind racing with possibilities. "Ain't no way she walkin' away clean."

Jasmine picked up her phone and dialed Dani. The phone rang twice before Dani answered, her voice cautious. "What's up, Jas? You good?"

"No, I ain't good," Jasmine snapped, her voice sharp. "Rico dropped some shit on me. Told me Sharice workin' with some dude named Dwayne. You heard that name before?"

Dani was silent for a moment before sighing. "Yeah, I heard it. Word is he used to be a cop, got caught up in some mess, and now he runnin' his own little game. Been sniffin' 'round boosters for months."

Jasmine's jaw tightened. "So this Dwayne been usin' Sharice to get to me? That what you sayin'?"

"Sounds like it," Dani admitted. "You gotta move smart, Jas. He playin' chess while you runnin' through the streets like it's checkers."

Jasmine let out a bitter laugh. "Yeah, well, he picked the wrong bitch to mess with. And Sharice? She dead to me."

"What you plannin'?" Dani asked, her tone wary.

"Somethin' she'll never forget," Jasmine replied, her voice cold. "You in?"

Dani hesitated but eventually said, "You know I got you. Just don't get too reckless."

The first step was gathering intel. Jasmine couldn't move on Sharice until she knew where she was hiding and what she was up to. She hit the streets, keeping her hood low and her business quieter than a whisper. The block was still buzzing about her, but most people didn't know what was really going down.

At the bodega, she leaned on the counter, her eyes scanning the store. "Yo, Rico," she called out, her voice low. "That address you gave me, it solid?"

Rico smirked from behind the counter, his gold tooth catching the light. "Far as I know. She been seen around there a few times. Why? You plannin' somethin'?"

"Don't worry 'bout it," Jasmine said, slipping him a few bills. "Just make sure it stay between us."

Rico nodded, pocketing the money. "Aight, but watch your back. Streets ain't friendly right now."

"Tell me somethin' I don't know," Jasmine muttered, grabbing her smokes and heading out.

Jasmine parked a block away from the address Rico had given her, her heart pounding as she scoped out the place. It was a rundown apartment building, the kind where the walls were thin, and the tenants didn't ask questions. Perfect for someone like Sharice.

She waited, her eyes glued to the entrance. Hours passed, and Jasmine's patience wore thin. Just as she was about to give up, the door opened, and Sharice stepped out, her long red weave flowing in the night breeze. She was laughing, her phone pressed to her ear, acting like she didn't have a care in the world.

Jasmine's grip tightened on the steering wheel. "Bitch," she hissed under her breath. She watched as Sharice walked to a car and got in, her demeanor casual. Jasmine waited a beat before starting her engine and following at a distance.

The trail led Jasmine to a small club on the edge of the city, the kind of place where hustlers mixed with wanna-be rappers and the drinks were always watered down. Jasmine parked across the street, watching as Sharice disappeared inside.

"Time to make my move," Jasmine muttered, pulling her hood up and stepping out of the car.

The club was dark and crowded, the bass from the speakers shaking the walls. Jasmine slipped through the crowd, keeping her eyes on Sharice, who was perched at the bar, chatting with a man in a leather jacket. Jasmine didn't recognize him, but she didn't need to. He wasn't her target.

She waited, biding her time, until Sharice stepped away, heading toward the restroom. Jasmine followed, her heart pounding with anger and adrenaline.

When the restroom door closed, Jasmine pushed it open, her footsteps echoing in the tiled room. Sharice was at the sink, fixing her lipstick in the mirror. She froze when she saw Jasmine's reflection.

"Jas?" Sharice said, her voice shaky. "What you doin' here?"

Jasmine slammed the door shut, locking it behind her. "You really gon' ask me that? After what you did?"

"I don't know what you talkin' 'bout," Sharice stammered, backing away from the sink.

"Don't play dumb bitch," Jasmine snapped, her voice cold. "You sold me out to that cop-wannabe Dwayne. You the reason the last job went left."

"I didn't have a choice!" Sharice cried, her back hitting the wall. "He had dirt on me, Jas. He said he'd lock me up if I didn't help him."

Jasmine's hands clenched into fists. "So you thought throwin' me under the bus was the move? After everything we been through?"

Tears welled up in Sharice's eyes. "I'm sorry, Jas. I didn't mean for it to go this far."

"Sorry don't mean shit," Jasmine said, her voice laced with venom. "You made your choice. Now you gotta live with it."

Sharice slid to the floor, her face buried in her hands. Jasmine stood over her, the rage boiling inside her. She wanted to do more, to make Sharice feel every ounce of pain she'd caused, but she held back. There were bigger fish to fry Dwayne.

"This ain't over," Jasmine said, her voice low and dangerous. "But right now, I got bigger problems than you. Pray you don't see me again."

With that, Jasmine turned and walked out of the restroom, leaving Sharice sobbing on the floor.

Back in her car, Jasmine lit a cigarette, her hands still trembling. She'd confronted Sharice, but the fire in her gut hadn't gone out. She needed to deal with Dwayne, the man pulling all the strings. But she couldn't rush it. She had to be smart, calculated.

As she drove off, her phone buzzed with a message from Dani: **"Heard somethin' 'bout Dwayne. Call me."**

Jasmine exhaled, the smoke curling around her. "Your move, Dwayne," she muttered, gripping the wheel. "Let's see how this game end."

The night was dark, the streets colder than ever, but Jasmine was ready. Revenge wasn't just a plan it was her survival.

Chapter 16: Dwayne's Trap

The early morning light barely touched the gritty streets as Jasmine paced her small motel room, her mind racing. She was careful now too many close calls had made her paranoid. She kept her routes random, stayed off her phone unless absolutely necessary, and avoided anyone who could tie her back to the game. But something still felt off, like the walls were closing in. And Dwayne? That name stayed in her head like a bad song on repeat.

"Somethin' ain't right," she muttered, staring at the cheap wallpaper like it held answers.

Her phone buzzed, breaking her thoughts. It was a text from Dani: **"Got a spot for a quick grab. Easy money. You down?"**

Jasmine frowned, her gut screaming to stay put. But the money was running out, and she needed a win. **"Send me the details,"** she replied, already regretting it.

Across town, Dwayne sat at his desk, his face lit by the glow of surveillance monitors. The footage from the jewelry store was playing on a loop, but his focus was on something else entirely a small envelope sitting on the desk in front of him.

Inside was fake evidence: doctored receipts, bogus witness statements, and even a grainy photo of Jasmine. It was all part of his plan. He didn't need to catch her in the act. He just needed the cops to believe she'd been there.

"She thinks she's slick," he muttered, a wicked grin spreading across his face. "But I'm always one step ahead."

Dwayne had tipped off the police about a so-called theft ring targeting high-end boutiques. The setup was simple: plant the evidence, call it in, and sit back while the system did his dirty work.

Jasmine pulled into the parking lot of an upscale boutique, her hood pulled low. Dani had said it was an easy grab a few items, quick in and out. But as Jasmine stepped inside, her nerves buzzed. The air felt thick, like the place was holding its breath.

The clerk behind the counter eyed her suspiciously, her smile too tight. Jasmine kept her head down, browsing the racks, but her gut was screaming. She glanced toward the back of the store, spotting a security camera pointed directly at her.

"This don't feel right," she muttered under her breath, heading for the door.

Before she could make it, two cops stepped inside, blocking her exit. "Ma'am, we need to talk," one of them said, his tone firm but rehearsed.

Jasmine froze, her heart slamming against her ribs. "Talk about what?" she asked, her voice steady despite the panic rising in her chest.

"Come with us," the other officer said, motioning toward the door. "Now."

The interrogation room was cold and sterile, the fluorescent lights buzzing overhead. Jasmine sat across from two detectives, her hands cuffed in front of her. They'd been hammering her with questions for hours, but she wasn't giving them anything.

"You're wasting your time," she said, leaning back in the chair. "I ain't done nothin'."

"Really?" one of the detectives sneered, sliding a stack of papers across the table. "These receipts say otherwise. And this picture?" He tapped on a grainy photo of a woman who looked a lot like Jasmine. "Pretty damning."

Jasmine's stomach turned, but she kept her face neutral. "That ain't me."

"Witnesses say it is," the detective replied, his tone smug. "You've been sloppy, Ms. Carter. Real sloppy."

Jasmine clenched her fists under the table. This was a setup she could feel it. But proving it was another story.

Meanwhile, Dani was pacing her apartment, her phone glued to her ear. "You serious?" she snapped into the receiver. "They got her locked up?"

The voice on the other end, low and gravelly, belonged to Black. "Yeah. Word is she got caught slippin'. But it don't add up. Jas don't move like that."

"She ain't do it," Dani said firmly. "Somebody settin' her up."

"Then we gotta get her out," Black replied. "I'll handle the bail. You just keep your head down."

Dani exhaled, relief washing over her. "Aight. Thanks, Black."

Hours later, Jasmine was escorted out of the holding cell, her wrists aching from the cuffs. The officer at the desk handed her a plastic bag with her belongings and a curt nod.

"Someone posted bail," he said, his tone clipped.

Jasmine didn't ask who. She just wanted to get out of there.

As she stepped outside, the cool night air hit her like a slap. A sleek black SUV idled at the curb, and the passenger window rolled down to reveal Black sitting behind the wheel.

"Get in," he said, his voice low.

Jasmine slid into the passenger seat, her body tense. "You did this?"

"Had to," Black replied, pulling away from the curb. "Can't have my people sittin' in a cell."

Jasmine stared out the window, her jaw tight. "They framed me. Had fake papers, fake pictures. All of it."

"I heard," Black said. "And I think I know who's behind it."

"Dwayne," Jasmine muttered, her voice dripping with venom.

Black nodded. "Yeah. Word is he been pullin' strings for a minute, tryin' to take you down."

Jasmine's hands clenched into fists. "He wanna play games? Fine. But he better be ready, 'cause I'm comin' for him."

Back at the motel, Jasmine paced the room, her mind racing. She couldn't trust anyone now not even Dani. The setup had been too clean, too perfect. Dwayne had resources, and he wasn't afraid to use them.

But Jasmine wasn't going to let him win. She pulled out a notebook and began scribbling names, places, and details. If she was going to take Dwayne down, she needed to be smarter, faster, and more ruthless than he was.

Her phone buzzed, a text from Dani: **"You good?"**

Jasmine stared at the screen for a long moment before replying: **"I will be. Just lay low for now."**

Meanwhile, Dwayne sat in his office, sipping a glass of whiskey as he reviewed the day's events. Jasmine might have gotten out on bail, but the damage was done. The cops were circling like vultures.

"She ain't got much left," he muttered to himself, a smug grin on his face. "Just a matter of time now."

But Dwayne underestimated Jasmine. The game was far from over, and she was already plotting her next move.

The streets were cold, the stakes high, and Jasmine was ready to play dirty. She didn't just want revenge she wanted to burn it all down.

Chapter 17: Street Justice

The bass from the club shook the ground like a heartbeat, the walls alive with the sound of music and chaos. Inside, the air was thick with smoke, sweat, and cheap cologne. Jasmine stepped through the door, her hood pulled low over her face, her sharp eyes scanning the crowd. The strobe lights flickered, casting jagged shadows over the packed dance floor.

This was the spot, where the streets came to floss, where the hustlers rubbed shoulders with the dealers, and the liars danced with the desperate. And tonight, Jasmine wasn't here to party she was hunting.

Her jaw clenched as she moved toward the bar, her mind replaying the whispers she'd heard earlier that day. Sharice was here. The same Sharice who'd set her up, left her for dead, and disappeared like she didn't owe Jasmine answers.

"She bold as hell, comin' out here like she ain't got enemies," Jasmine muttered under her breath, her hand tightening around the strap of her purse. "Bet."

Sharice was posted near the VIP section, laughing loud enough to drown out the music. Her long red weave was flawless, her glittering dress catching the light with every move. She held a drink in one hand, her nails sharp and painted gold, while the other hand rested on the arm of some dude Jasmine didn't recognize.

Jasmine's blood boiled at the sight. She'd been laying low, ducking cops, and scrambling for every dollar, while Sharice was out here like nothing happened. Like betrayal wasn't written all over her.

"Nah," Jasmine muttered, sliding up to the bar. "She don't get to walk away from this."

"Yo, can I get a shot?" Jasmine said to the bartender, keeping her tone casual. Her eyes never left Sharice, watching every laugh, every move, every fake-ass smile. Jasmine knew she couldn't just walk up on her. Not yet. She needed to wait for the perfect moment.

"Who you starin' at like that?" a voice said next to her.

Jasmine turned to see Dani leaning on the bar, her expression a mix of concern and curiosity.

"Sharice," Jasmine said flatly, nodding toward the VIP section.

Dani followed her gaze, her face hardening. "What you plannin', Jas? Don't do nothin' stupid."

"Stupid?" Jasmine snapped, her voice low but sharp. "She the one who crossed me. She the reason I been runnin' like a damn fugitive."

"I get it," Dani said, her tone steady. "But this ain't the place. Too many eyes."

"I don't care," Jasmine hissed, slamming her empty glass on the bar. "She gotta feel what I felt."

Jasmine didn't wait for Dani's approval. She moved through the crowd, her steps deliberate, her pulse pounding in her ears. By the time Sharice noticed her, it was too late.

"Well, well," Jasmine said, her voice cutting through the noise. "Look who livin' her best life."

Sharice's laughter died instantly, her drink freezing halfway to her lips. Her eyes widened, then narrowed, as she realized who was standing in front of her.

"Jas," she said, her voice tight. "What you doin' here?"

"What *I'm* doin' here?" Jasmine repeated, her tone mocking. "The real question is, what the hell you doin'? Fucking Rat!"

Sharice tried to play it cool, leaning back in her chair. "I don't know what you talkin' 'bout."

"Don't play dumb, Sharice," Jasmine snapped, stepping closer. "You set me up damn coward."

The crowd around them started to notice, the noise dying down as people turned to watch. Sharice shifted uncomfortably, her bravado slipping.

"I didn't have a choice, Jas," Sharice said, her voice low. "You don't know what he had on me."

"I don't give a damn what he had on you!" Jasmine yelled, her voice slicing through the air. "You supposed to be my girl, and you sold me out for what? To save your own ass?"

Sharice stood, her heels clicking on the tile as she squared up to Jasmine. "You think you so perfect?" she shot back, her voice trembling with anger. "You think you wouldn't do the same if it was you? Dwayne had me cornered. I had to make a move!"

"You made the wrong one," Jasmine growled, her fists clenching at her sides. "And now you gon' pay for it."

Sharice laughed bitterly, her hands on her hips. "You ain't gon' do nothin', Jas. You all talk."

That was it. Jasmine snapped.

She lunged at Sharice, grabbing her by the front of her dress and yanking her forward. The crowd erupted in chaos as the two women tumbled to the floor, fists flying and curses spilling from their lips.

"You think I won't?" Jasmine screamed, her voice raw with rage. "You think this a game?"

Sharice clawed at Jasmine, her nails digging into her arm as she fought to push her off. "Get the hell off me!" she shouted, her voice cracking.

The bouncers rushed in, pulling the women apart, but not before Jasmine landed one last punch, splitting Sharice's lip.

By the time Jasmine was dragged outside, her chest was heaving, her adrenaline still pumping. Dani was waiting for her by the curb, her face a mixture of disbelief and disappointment.

"What the hell was that, Jas?" Dani said, grabbing her arm.

"She deserved it," Jasmine spat, her lip curled. "After everything she did to me, she lucky I didn't end her right there."

"And now what?" Dani snapped. "You think she just gon' let this slide? Sharice ain't the type to take an ass-whoopin' and keep quiet."

Jasmine pulled her arm free, her face hard. "Let her come. I'm ready."

Back inside, Sharice sat slumped in a booth, her lip bleeding and her pride shattered. Her hands trembled as she held a napkin to her face, her mind racing with thoughts of revenge.

"She think this over?" Sharice muttered to herself, her voice shaking with rage. "Nah. It's just gettin' started."

Jasmine walked down the empty street, her hood pulled up, her fists still clenched. The cold night air did little to cool the fire burning inside her. She knew she'd made a scene, knew the streets would be buzzing with what happened. But she didn't care. Sharice had it coming.

Her phone buzzed in her pocket. It was a text from an unknown number: **"You're losing control. Watch yourself."**

Jasmine stared at the message, her jaw tightening. The game was getting more dangerous, the stakes higher. But Jasmine wasn't backing down.

Not now. Not ever.

Chapter 18: The Price of the Game

The weak sunlight of morning spilled through the thin curtains of Jasmine's apartment. Back at home because she didn't have much more money to spend on hotel rooms. She sat on the worn couch, her kids nestled beside her. The tree, barely decorated and slightly lopsided, stood in the corner like a silent witness to the chaos she'd survived.

Jasmine watched them with a mix of relief and guilt. She was here alive, free, and able to see their smiles. But the weight of everything she'd done pressed heavy on her chest. The stolen goods, the lies, the betrayals it was all still there, lingering like a shadow.

"Ma, look!" her youngest, Jada, squealed, holding up a doll Jasmine had snagged during one of her runs. The girl's joy was pure, untainted by the dark reality of how it came to be.

"That's nice, baby," Jasmine said, forcing a smile. She stroked Jada's hair, her fingers trembling slightly.

Jada giggled, running to show her brother. Jasmine leaned back, her eyes closing for a moment. For now, they were happy. For now, they were safe. But she couldn't shake the thought: *How long can this last?*

The knock on the door came around mid-morning, sharp and unexpected. Jasmine tensed, her mind instantly jumping to worst-case scenarios. She moved to the door cautiously, peering through the peephole.

It was Mrs. Lorraine from down the hall, her arms full of food. Behind her stood two other neighbors, one holding a box of toys, the other with a tray of cookies.

Jasmine hesitated before opening the door. "Uh, hey, Miss Lorraine. What's all this?"

"Happy Holidays, Jas," the older woman said with a warm smile. "Thought you and the kids could use a lil' somethin'. The building chipped in."

Jasmine blinked, her throat tightening. She hadn't expected this. "Y'all ain't have to do all that..."

"Girl, hush," Mrs. Lorraine said, pushing past her into the apartment. The others followed, setting the food and gifts on the table. "We know it's been rough on you and you been goin thru some things. Everybody need a lil' help sometimes."

Jasmine stood frozen, watching as the neighbors fussed over the kids, their laughter filling the small apartment. It was a stark contrast to the violence and fear she'd been living in. For the first time in weeks, the tension in her shoulders eased slightly.

"Thank you," she said finally, her voice soft. "For real."

Mrs. Lorraine patted her arm. "You just keep takin' care of them babies, Jasmine. That's what matters."

Across town, the sterile walls of the hospital were a far cry from the festive holiday chaos of Jasmine's apartment. Dwayne lay in a hospital bed, his leg bandaged and elevated and recovering from surgery for a gunshot wound to the stomach. He had tried to stop some holiday shoplifters one had pulled out a gun and shot him to keep him from chasing them so they could get away.

He stared groggy at the ceiling, his jaw tight, replaying the events in his mind.

A nurse entered the room, her expression neutral as she checked his vitals. "You're lucky to be alive," she said, her tone curt. "Should be grateful."

"Grateful?" Dwayne sneered, his eyes narrowing. "For what?

The nurse rolled her eyes and left without another word. Dwayne didn't care. He wasn't here to make friends. His obsession burned hotter now, fueled by humiliation and unfinished business.

He reached for his phone on the bedside table, scrolling through his contacts until he found the name he was looking for. Pressing buttons, his fingers drumming against the bedrail.

Back at the apartment, Jasmine sat at the kitchen table, the noise of her kids and neighbors fading into the background. She stared at the pile of food and gifts, her mind a whirlwind of thoughts. The hustle had given her moments like this, fleeting glimpses of normalcy, but it had also taken so much.

Her phone buzzed on the counter. She picked it up hesitantly, her heart sinking when she saw the message.

"This ain't over. Watch your back."

She didn't need to guess who it was. Dwayne wasn't going to let this go.

Jasmine gritted her teeth, her anger bubbling to the surface. She was tired she was done with this shit!

For the first time, she let herself imagine a different life. A life where she wasn't running, where her kids didn't have to grow up with the struggling. It felt impossible, but the thought lingered, a flicker of hope in the darkness.

As the night wore on, in her apartment, the sound of her kids' laughter pulling her from her thoughts.

"Everything good?" the older woman asked, her tone gentle.

"Yeah," Jasmine said, her voice quiet. "Thanks again, Miss Lorraine."

She sat on the couch, pulling her kids close. For now, they were safe. For now, they had each other. And for Jasmine, that was enough.

But deep down, she knew the game wasn't over. Dwayne was still out there, and the streets were still watching. The price of the hustle had been steep, and it wasn't done collecting.

Jasmine made a silent vow: whatever came next, she'd be ready.

And she wasn't going down without a fight.

Don't miss out!

Visit the website below and you can sign up to receive emails whenever Rachael Reed publishes a new book. There's no charge and no obligation.

https://books2read.com/r/B-A-WXARB-TYPKF

BOOKS 2 READ

Connecting independent readers to independent writers.

Did you love *Hustlin Through the Holidays*? Then you should read *Cartel Bloodline*[1] by Rachael Reed!

Cartel Bloodline: A Tale of Love, Betrayal, and Survival in the Miami Underworld

In the ruthless streets of Miami, where the Cartel controls eighty percent of the cocaine flowing through the port, power is everything, and trust is a luxury no one can afford. When the most feared gangster, Antonio Brown, falls, he leaves behind a legacy that's more explosive than anyone could've imagined. His death unearths a hidden secret—an illegitimate son, Antonio Lewis, who's about to step into a world where loyalty is bought with blood and betrayal lurks around every corner.

Antonio Lewis, raised far from the chaos of Miami's underworld, gets pulled into the Cartel's deadly embrace when he learns of his father's

---

1. https://books2read.com/u/4jpKMk

2. https://books2read.com/u/4jpKMk

empire. Thrown into a cutthroat game where every ally is a potential enemy, Antonio must navigate the treacherous waters of his father's legacy, battling for his place in the empire while uncovering the dark secrets that threaten to consume him.

Lea, a deadly beauty with a heart of steel, leads The Get Money Girls, a crew of contract killers who live by their own rules. When her cousin falls in a botched hit on the Cartel, Lea vows revenge, unaware that her heart would soon become entangled with the enemy. Antonio and Lea's worlds collide in a storm of passion and deceit, their forbidden love a ticking time bomb ready to explode.

As alliances crumble and enemies close in, Antonio and Lea must face the ultimate betrayal from within their ranks. The lines between love and loyalty blur, and survival becomes a deadly game of cat and mouse. The streets of Miami become a battlefield, where every decision could mean life or death, and the only way out is to fight until the last breath.

Will Antonio rise to claim his father's throne, or will the legacy of the Cartel drag him down into the abyss? Can Lea reconcile her thirst for vengeance with the love that binds her to Antonio, or will the secrets they uncover tear them apart forever?

Cartel Bloodline is a gritty, suspense-filled journey through the dark underbelly of Miami, where power is fleeting, love is dangerous, and the ultimate betrayal could come from the person you trust the most. In this world, nothing is as it seems, and the streets never forget.

Also by Rachael Reed

Sis
Sis 2 Blood on the Streets

Standalone
Codefendant
Codefendant
Once a Cheater
Once a Cheater
Passport Bro
What Happens in Prison
Preference
Sprinkle Sprinkle
Championship Bad
Street Exodus
Street Exodus
Street Royalty
Pawns of Power
SIS
Cartel Bloodline
Get Money Girls
Skip the Games
Til Death Do Us Part

Backpage Hustle
Link in Bio
The Virgin and The Kingpin
A Gangsta's Heart
Boosters
Can't Turn a Hoe Into a Housewife
Better you Than Me
Wig Dealer: How to Start Your wig Business
Trail Ride Blues
Demure Diva
Queen of the Carnival
Caribbean Carnival Hoe
How to Glow Up! Make 2025 Your Best Year
How to Lose 10 Pounds in a Month
What is Project 2025? The Easy to Understand Guide
What Is A Tariff
Natural Hair Growth Oil with 50 Recipes
Regrow Hair Naturally in 3 Weeks
Hustlin Through the Holidays

www.ingramcontent.com/pod-product-compliance
Lightning Source LLC
Chambersburg PA
CBHW022055150726
47990CB00003B/1090